Being a Good Citizen

Andrew McNamara

Real Life Readers™

Rosen Classroom™

New York

Published in 2009 by The Rosen Publishing Group, Inc.
29 East 21st Street, New York, NY 10010

Book Design: Michael J. Flynn

Photo Credits: Cover (workers) © Yellow Dog Productions/The Image Bank/Getty Images; cover (American flag), pp. 3 (American flag), 4 (American flag), 7 (American flag), 8 (American flag), 11 (American flag), 12 (American flag), 15 (American flag), 16 (American flag) © akva/Shutterstock; p. 5 © Glenda M. Powers/Shutterstock; p. 6 © Image Source/Getty Images; p. 9 © maigi/Shutterstock; p. 10 © Elena Elisseeva/Shutterstock; p. 11 (sign) © bhathaway/Shutterstock; p. 13 © Robert Laberge/Getty Images Sport/Getty Images.

ISBN: 978-1-4358-0071-7
6-pack ISBN: 978-1-4358-0072-4

Manufactured in the United States of America

Word Count: 164

Contents

What Is a Citizen?

A **citizen** is a person who has the **right** to live in a country.
Good citizens are people who help their country.
There are many ways to be a good citizen.

VOTE
FOR
SMITH
SMITH
for
PRESIDENT
BALLOTS
SMITH

VOTING

Good citizens **vote** for community leaders.
You can be a good citizen when you vote
for your school leaders.
Good citizens are often good leaders.
You can ask people to vote for you, too!

Keeping Our Community Clean

Good citizens follow community **rules**.

Some community rules help keep

our neighborhoods clean.

A rule may tell us not to litter and to **recycle**

our waste.

Some good citizens clean their neighborhoods.

Community Rules

recycle waste → keeps community clean

don't litter → keeps community clean

ride on bike path → keeps community safe

cross at crosswalk → keeps community safe

Keeping Our Community Safe

Some community rules help keep
our neighborhoods safe.
A rule may tell us to ride on a bike path
or cross the street only at a **crosswalk**.
Can you think of another community rule?

Ways to Help

Good citizens are good helpers.
You can help your older neighbors.
You can help plant a garden or
even help build a house!
What other things can you do
to help your community?

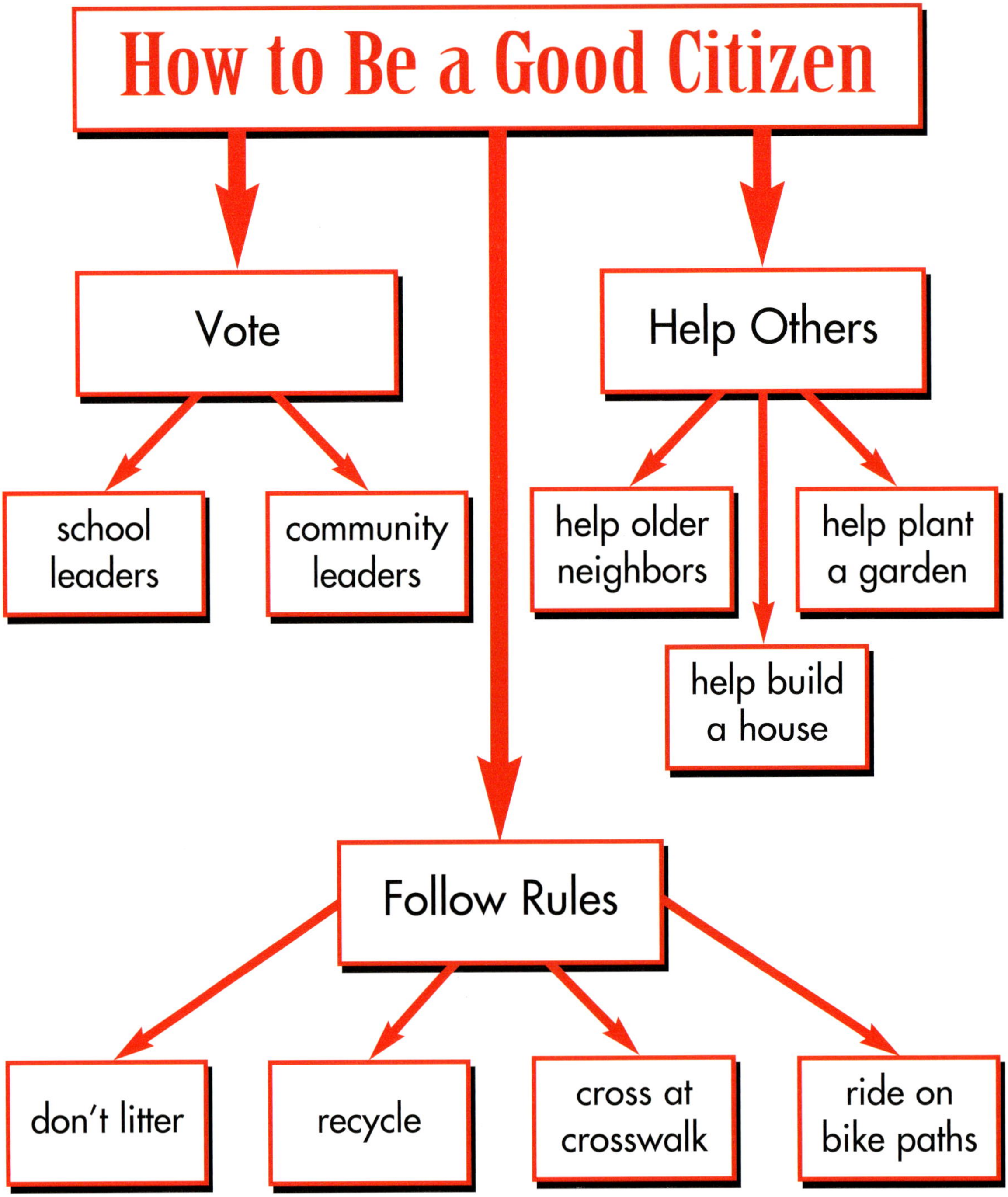
How to Be a Good Citizen
Vote
school leaders
community leaders
Help Others
help older neighbors
help plant a garden
help build a house
Follow Rules
don't litter
recycle
cross at crosswalk
ride on bike paths

GLOSSARY

citizen (SIH-tuh-zuhn) A person who has a right to live in a country or other community.

crosswalk (KROS-wahk) A place marked on a street where people can cross safely.

recycle (ree-SY-kuhl) To use something again in a different way.

right (RYT) Something that someone is able to have or do.

rule (ROOL) Something that tells us how to act.

vote (VOHT) To choose someone or something.

INDEX